C

**THIS BOOK
BELONGS TO**

This edition published by HarperCollins Publishers Ltd 1999 for Silverdale Books
An imprint of Bookmart Ltd
Registered Number 2372865
Trading as Bookmart Limited
Desford Rd, Enderby, Leicester, LE9 5AD
First published 1954 by Sampson Lowe
© Darrell Waters Limited 1954 as to all text and illustrations
Enid Blyton's signature mark and the word 'NODDY' are Registered
Trade Marks of Enid Blyton Ltd
All rights reserved
ISBN 0 26 167241-X
Printed and bound in Italy

NODDY GETS INTO TROUBLE

BY Enid Blyton

CONTENTS

NODDY WAVED HIS HAND AT A SUNBEAM

1

EARLY IN THE MORNING

NODDY woke up one morning and found the sun streaming in at his window. He nodded his head happily.

"I think it's going to be
A lucky day for me!"

he sang to himself, and waved his hands at a sunbeam dancing on the ceiling.

He jumped out of bed and did a little dance round the room. The sun shone warmly in, and Noddy held out his hands to it.

"Ooooh—you *are* lovely and warm, Mr Sun! How kind of you to shine on my lucky day!"

Noddy dressed himself, humming like a bumble bee all the time, he felt so happy. He put his little blue hat on his head and the bell jingled merrily.

"Why even you can sing.
Jingle-jingle-jing!"

said Noddy. "Dear me, I am very clever at making up little songs today. I wish Big-Ears were here to listen. He would laugh and clap his hands. Dear Big-Ears, how lucky I am to have him for a friend."

He got his breakfast, and the milkman came just at the right moment as Noddy was putting his empty milk-jug on the table.

"Milko!" he called, and handed the milk through the window, smiling at little Noddy. Noddy took it, and paid for it as usual by letting the milkman tap his head and make it nod so fast that he couldn't even speak!

"Thanks," said the milkman. "I wish I had a head like yours, Noddy. Mine keeps quite still. It must be exciting to have one like yours."

Noddy nodded at the milkman. "Yes," he said. "And today it's nodding more than ever because I feel it's my lucky day. Something's going to happen, I know it is!"

"Well, I hope it's something nice, that's all," said the milkman. "Good-day to you, little

Noddy." Off he went, and Noddy heard him calling, "Milko! Milko!" all down the road.

Noddy was still feeling that it was his lucky day when he began his breakfast. He was rather surprised to find that his boiled egg didn't taste very nice. He made a face.

"Pooh! You don't smell very nice, egg—and you don't taste nice. I shan't eat you!"

He pushed his egg to the other side of the table. "You're not a lucky egg," he said. "And you *should* have been on my lucky day."

He went out to get his little car—and oh dear, oh dear—one of the tyres was flat!

"Well! Anyone would think this was my unlucky day! What do you mean by this, car?"

"Parp-parp," said the car sadly. It didn't like having a flat tyre.

"I'm beginning to feel cross," said little Noddy. "Things shouldn't go wrong on my lucky day. Bother, bother, bother. Hallo—who's this coming up my garden path?"

2

HALLO, MR PLOD!

IT was Mr Plod the policeman coming up the path. He looked rather solemn.

"Hallo!" said Noddy. "Do you want me to take you anywhere in my car, Mr Plod?"

"No," said Mr Plod. "I've come to ask you where you were in the middle of last night, Noddy."

"In bed, of course," said Noddy, alarmed. "Why?"

"Because somebody went to Miss Fluffy Cat's house, and climbed in at a window and took some jam tarts, a meat pie and a chocolate cake from her larder," said Mr Plod, looking at a list in his notebook.

"Goodness! What a shocking thing to do!" said Noddy. "But surely—surely you don't think *I* did it, Mr Plod? You know I couldn't possibly be so bad."

"Well—Miss Fluffy Cat is very surprised, but she *does* think you stole her tarts and pie and cake," said Mr Plod.

"Why does she?" cried Noddy. "She's horrid to say that. I'll never, never take her out in my car again, never, never, never, never, nev . . ."

"That's enough nevers," said Mr Plod. "Miss Fluffy Cat heard the jingling of a little bell as the thief climbed out of the window and ran

away. And you're the only one in Toyland who jingles when he walks, Noddy, because you've a bell on the end of your hat."

Noddy's head nodded fiercely at Mr Plod, and his bell jingled loudly and fiercely too. "I didn't go to Miss Fluffy

11

Cat's in the night," he said. "I wouldn't, I wouldn't, I wouldn't."

"That's enough wouldn'ts," said Mr Plod, frowning. He shut his notebook and looked sternly at poor Noddy.

"Suppose I look in your larder?" he said.

"Yes—you come and look!" said Noddy, and he pulled Mr Plod into his house and opened the little larder door. "See—there isn't a jam tart or a meat pie or a cake!"

"What are those crumbs?" said Mr Plod, picking up some dark brown crumbs that lay on the larder shelf. He sniffed at them. "Chocolate cake crumbs! Noddy, are you telling the truth?"

"Of course I am!" said Noddy. "I had a few chocolate buns yesterday, and those must be the crumbs. I tell you I *didn't* steal from Miss Fluffy Cat's larder. I didn't, I didn't, I didn't."

"That's enough didn'ts," said Mr Plod. "Well—I shan't say any more to you just now, little Noddy. If you didn't go to Miss Fluffy Cat's, I'm glad—but if you did—well, LOOK OUT!"

12

"WHAT ARE THOSE CRUMBS?" SAID MR PLOD

3

NOBODY LOVES NODDY

NODDY was very, very upset when Mr Plod had gone. He sat on the larder floor and cried. "I thought it was my lucky day. But it's not. Mr Plod was horrid to me. I don't like him any more. I DIDN'T go to Miss Fluffy Cat's, unless I walked in my sleep."

Noddy wiped his eyes and thought hard. "Could I have walked in my sleep? People do sometimes. No, I couldn't have because I would fall over things and wake up. And if I had taken the pie and the tarts and the cake they would be here in my larder. And they're not."

He got up and went to his car. He pumped up the flat tyre. He didn't sing, or hum, or think it was his lucky day. It certainly wasn't!

14

He took his little car out into the village and looked about for passengers. But nobody hailed him. Nobody even called, "Good morning! How are you, little Noddy?"

"Why does everyone turn away from me?" wondered Noddy. "Hey, Mr Wobbly-Man! How are your wobbles?"

Mr Wobbly-Man didn't seem to hear. He wobbled away round a corner and Noddy stared after him.

"Oh dear! Why doesn't anyone speak to me? Surely Miss Fluffy Cat hasn't told them she thinks I went to her house in the middle of the night?"

But that was just what Miss Fluffy Cat had done! What a shame! Now they thought little Noddy was very, very naughty, and they didn't want to smile at him or talk to him. They wouldn't even ride in his car, so he didn't get a single passenger all that day.

He was very sad when he put his car away that evening. "Nobody loves me any more," he told the car. "I think I'd better go and tell Big-Ears about it tomorrow. I'm sure *he* will still love me."

Now the next morning Noddy was just getting dressed when a loud knock came at his door. Blam-blam!

He jumped. Goodness—who was that so early in the morning? He put his head out of the window.

It was Mr Plod, standing on the door-step with his notebook in his hand, looking very stern indeed. Noddy felt afraid. "I don't think I will open the door to him," he thought. "He looks so fierce."

"Good morning, Mr Plod. Is there anything I can do for you?"

IT WAS MR PLOD STANDING ON THE DOOR-STEP

"Open the door," said Mr Plod. "I have something to say to you, little Noddy."

"Say it out there," said Noddy, his head nodding in fright. "I'm not going to open the door. Your face doesn't look kind this morning."

"Don't be silly, Noddy," said Mr Plod. "I've come to ask you where you were last night."

"What, *again*?" said Noddy, in alarm. "I was in bed all night except when my feet slid out from the blankets and I got out to put them back."

"Noddy—somebody with a jingling bell got into Mr Wobbly-Man's house last night and took a box of ginger biscuits," said Mr Plod, sternly.

"Well, it wasn't ME!" said Noddy, and slammed the window shut. He burst into tears. "Oh, I'm so unhappy! I didn't get into anyone's house, I didn't, I didn't! Go away, Mr Plod! Don't take me to prison. I'm a good little Noddy. I am, I am, I am!"

4

WHERE IS BIG-EARS?

MR Plod went away, looking very fierce. Noddy finished dressing himself and ran to get his car. Quick, quick, before Mr Plod comes back again! Hurry, car, hurry to Big-Ears!

The car hurried. It bumped over stones and splashed through puddles, it swung round corners and it hooted at everything in its way. It even hooted at the lamp-post at the bottom of the road. But the lamp-post didn't get out of the way, of course.

"Parp-parp!" hooted the little car. "Here comes Noddy, parp-parp!"

They went into the wood and at last came to Big-Ears' toadstool house. Noddy jumped out and ran to the door. He knocked on it loudly.

"Big-Ears, Big-Ears, it's me, little Noddy. I want you, Big-Ears. Open the door quickly!"

But the door didn't open. It stayed shut, and Noddy stared at it, very worried. Was Big-Ears cross too? Did he believe what Miss Fluffy Cat

and Mr Wobbly-Man said? Noddy went to the window and looked in. Big-Ears, dear Big-Ears, where are you?

But there was nobody in the toadstool house, not even the cat. Noddy was surprised. It was early in the morning. Where had Big-Ears gone?

A small rabbit lolloped up and stared at Noddy.

"Hey!" said Noddy. "Where's Big-Ears?"

"Gone away," said the rabbit. "His brother Little-Ears is ill, so he's gone to look after him. He went in the middle of the night."

"Oh dear!" said poor Noddy. "Bother Little-Ears! Why did he get ill just when I want Big-Ears? Where does Little-Ears live, bunny?"

21

"*I* don't know!" said the rabbit, twitching his long ears. "Can you twitch *your* ears, Noddy?"

"Of course not. I'm not a silly rabbit," said Noddy. "Which way did Big-Ears go, bunny?"

But the rabbit didn't know. He twitched his nose and his ears at Noddy, and then tried to nod his head like him. But he couldn't.

"You can't twitch your ears and nose like a silly rabbit—and I can't nod my head like a silly Noddy!" said the bunny, with a squeal of laughter. He ran down his hole, still laughing, and Noddy glared at his bobbing white tail. He stamped his foot. "Everything's gone wrong! Nobody likes me any more. Mr Plod is very cross. Big-Ears has gone away just when I want him. NOW what am I to do?"

THE RABBIT TWITCHED HIS NOSE AND EARS AT NODDY

5

A SURPRISE FOR NODDY

NODDY got into his car and drove away again, feeling very upset. He looked about for passengers when he came to the village—but still nobody hailed him!

He saw Mr Monkey with a heavy case on his shoulder, and he stopped beside him. "Hey, Mr Monkey—do you want me to take you to the station?"

"No, thank you," said Mr Monkey. "I've heard strange things about you, Noddy. Very strange. I don't want to go in your car again."

24

Noddy drove off, his face very red. Oh dear, did people REALLY believe he had been to Miss Fluffy Cat's house and Mr Wobbly-Man's? Ah— there was Mr Tall-Bear, and he had some heavy parcels. Perhaps *he* would hire Noddy's car?

But Mr Tall-Bear wouldn't even *speak* to Noddy. He just made a face at him, which was very rude. Noddy drove off again, so worried that he almost ran over Mr Plod in the middle of the road. The car gave a sudden parp-parp, and Mr Plod almost jumped out of his skin.

"I'm sorry, I'm sorry, I'm sorry!" yelled Noddy, and swerved past the startled Mr Plod at top speed.

Nobody wanted him. Nobody spoke to him. When he passed the Noah's Ark animals walking two by two down the road, they all looked the other way—even Mr Noah looked away.

Noddy went home and put the car into the garage. He was very unhappy. He went into his little house and sat down. He put his face into his hands—and soon big tears trickled through his fingers.

"Nobody loves me! They think I'm bad. But I'm not, I'm not, I'm not. Oh, I do feel so lonely!"

Just then there was a little knock at the door—oh, a very tiny knock. Tap—tap—tap. Noddy didn't hear.

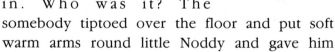

The door opened, very softly, and somebody looked in. Who was it? The somebody tiptoed over the floor and put soft warm arms round little Noddy and gave him

26

SOMEBODY GAVE NODDY SUCH A HUG!

such a hug! He looked up and who should it be but a dear little teddy bear in a pretty skirt and bonnet!

"It's you, Tessie Bear!" said Noddy, very pleased. "I didn't hear you come in. What a lovely hug you gave me! I was feeling so unhappy."

Tessie Bear smiled at Noddy shyly. She put her hand in her skirt pocket and pulled out her handkerchief. It was very small, but somehow she managed to wipe Noddy's eyes with it.

"What big tears you have!" she said. "My hanky is soaked! Noddy, what's the matter?"

Noddy looked at little Tessie. He often met her at Mrs Tubby Bear's, and he liked her.

"I'll tell you all about it," he said. "Hold my hand, Tessie. I shall feel better then. But first of all, tell me why you came in."

"I came to see my aunt, Mrs Tubby," said Tessie. "But she was out. So I thought I'd ask you to give her a message. I knocked but you didn't hear me, so I opened the door. And then I saw you sitting here, little Noddy—and you looked SO sad that I just had to hug you."

"It was a very, very nice hug," said Noddy. "And it made me feel better at once. Now listen and I'll tell you what's happened, Tessie Bear."

6

A GOOD LITTLE FRIEND

TESSIE Bear was a very good listener indeed. Noddy told her how Mr Plod had come to see him and had said that Mrs Fluffy Cat and Mr Wobbly-Man both thought he had got into their houses at night and stolen things to eat.

"But I didn't," said Noddy. "I didn't, I didn't, I didn't."

"Why did they think you did it?" asked Tessie.

"Oh, because the thief had a bell that jingled," said Noddy. "And I wear a hat with a jingly bell. Listen!"

He nodded his head and the bell jingled. Tessie listened and nodded her head too. But she hadn't a bell on her bonnet so she didn't jingle.

"I wish I jingled too," she said. "I do so love your bell, Noddy. How horrid of Miss Fluffy Cat and Mr Wobbly-Man to say that the thief was you. I shan't like them any more."

"Well, EVERYBODY believes I am the thief," said Noddy sadly, and his bell stopped jingling. "Nobody will speak to me. Mr Plod is waiting to take me to prison. Even Big-Ears has gone away, I don't know where. So I haven't a friend in the world."

"Yes, you have," said Tessie Bear, and she put her little paw into Noddy's hand. "I'm your friend. *I'll* speak to you. I know you couldn't possibly do a horrid thing, little Noddy."

"Oh! Are you really my friend?" said Noddy, in delight. "Oh, Tessie Bear! It's *so* nice to have someone loving me again. I've been so miserable. It's dreadful not to be loved, you know. I shan't mind now if people don't speak to me for weeks and weeks. I shan't mind if Mr Plod comes to fetch me and lock me up!"

"Oh no—that's silly, Noddy," said Tessie Bear. "Very silly. You *must* mind—you must find out who is pretending to be you, jingling a bell when he breaks into people's houses."

"But I can't," wailed Noddy. "How can I?"

"I've got a plan," said Tessie Bear. "Shall I make some cocoa, and then tell you about it?"

"Yes, let's have some cocoa—and there are some biscuits in that tin," said Noddy, his bell jingling once more. "Oh, I'm feeling happy again, Tessie. Let me reach down the cocoa tin; there you are!"

"OH! I'M FEELING HAPPY AGAIN, TESSIE," SAID NODDY

7

AT THE BELL-SHOP

TESSIE'S plan was a very good one. "Now,
listen, Noddy," she said. "It wasn't *your* bell
that jingled when the thief got into Miss Fluffy
Cat's—it was some other bell that the thief
bought so that he could pretend he was you.
Everybody knows when you are about, because
of your jingly bell."

"Yes. Go on, Tessie," said Noddy, listening
hard. "I do think you are clever."

"Well, the thief must have *bought* the bell,
mustn't he?" said Tessie. "So all we have to do

34

is to go to the bell-shop and find out who bought a bell like yours a little while ago!"

"Oh Tessie! How very clever you are!" said Noddy. "I wish I could buy brains like yours. Let's go to the bell-shop as soon as we have finished our cocoa. Have another biscuit?"

Well, when they had finished their cocoa Noddy got out his little car and he and Tessie Bear went off to the bell-shop in it. Noddy didn't care a bit now if everybody turned away and wouldn't speak to him—Tessie was in the car with him, for everyone to see. He had a friend after all!

The bell-shop was a lovely place, quite small, and hung with bells of every kind—big ones, small ones, some on ropes, some on handles, some like Noddy's bell that had to be sewn on to something.

There were bells to hang on reins, school bells, cow bells, bicycle bells and church bells. Noddy

35

began to ring them all. WHAT a noise!

The shop-keeper was a peculiar little wooden man with tufts of cotton wool sticking out of his ears. Noddy stared at him.

"Have you got ear-ache?" he said.

"No. I just get tired of the noise of bells, that's all," said the bell-man. "Do you want to buy one? I see you have a nice one on your hat."

"I don't want to buy one," said Noddy. "Though I really would like this great big one. DONG-DONG-DONG—doesn't it make a noise?"

"Don't," said the shop-keeper, stuffing more cotton wool into his ears.

"What we want to know is whether you have sold a bell lately that makes a jingly noise just like Noddy's," said Tessie Bear.

"Let me see—yes, I have," said the bell-man. "I sold one to each of the reindeer in the

36

THE BELL-SHOP WAS A LOVELY PLACE

Noah's Ark. They said they didn't feel like real reindeer unless they had bells that jingled.''

''So *they* came for bells!'' said Noddy.

''And I sold a bell to Mrs Sailor Doll for the little donkey she has for Susie Sailor Doll,'' said the shop-keeper.

''Did you really?'' said Noddy, wondering if Mrs Sailor Doll could possibly be the thief.

''And I sold a nice little bell to the clockwork mouse,'' said the bell-man. ''Goodness knows what *he* wanted one for. He doesn't usually want people to hear when he comes creeping along, he's a timid little thing.''

''Well, thank you,'' said Tessie Bear, and she took Noddy out of the bell-shop before he could ring a very big bell indeed.

38

8

THE REINDEER AND THE DONKEY

"NOW first we must go to the Ark and ask the reindeer a few things," said Tessie. "I expect reindeer like jam tarts and meat pies as much as anyone else!"

So off they drove to the Ark. They heard the jingling of bells as soon as they got there. It sounded just like Noddy's bell jingling!

"Have you been out at night lately?" asked Tessie, when they found the two wooden reindeer. They shook their heads in surprise, and their bells jingled loudly. They each had one round their necks.

"No," said both reindeer together. "How can we go out at night? You know that Mr Noah always locks the door of the Ark. Do you like our new bells? We feel like *real* reindeer now that we jingle. Perhaps Father Christmas will let us pull his sleigh next Christmas!"

Tessie and Noddy drove away, certain that it couldn't have been the reindeer's bells that Miss Fluffy Cat and Mr Wobbly-Man had heard.

"We'll go to Mrs Sailor Doll's house," said Noddy. "It isn't far away."

They soon came to it. It was a dear little house,

and its chimneys looked just like the funnels of a steamer, two set in a row.

"I wouldn't be surprised if Sailor Doll's house suddenly puffed smoke from its funnel-chimneys, and floated off over the garden," said Noddy.

Mrs Sailor Doll was surprised to see them, especially when she knew they had come

about the little donkey's bell.

"Oh, I don't think little Hee-Haw could climb in through anyone's window, at night," she said.

41

"Besides, he really doesn't like jam tarts or meat pies—he only likes carrots. Anyway, he has had a bad leg for a week, so he couldn't possibly get through a window."

Noddy and Tessie looked out of the window at little Hee-Haw. His bell jingled as he limped slowly over the grass.

"It couldn't be Hee-Haw," said Tessie. "Thank you, Mrs Sailor Doll, we'll go now."

So out they went, feeling disappointed. "There's only the clockwork mouse left," said Noddy. "And really, Tessie, he's so very timid that I'm quite sure he would never dare to go into anyone's house at night and steal things."

"I think that too," said Tessie sadly. "Oh, Noddy—my good idea wasn't very good after all. I'm SURE it wasn't the clockwork mouse."

"Let's go home again and have some more cocoa," said Noddy. "Or perhaps we could have lemonade this time. You might have another good idea, Tessie. Come along!"

NODDY AND TESSIE LOOKED OUT OF THE WINDOW

43

9

WHO HAS THE JINGLY BELL?

WELL, will you believe it, as they were driving back to Noddy's house they met the clockwork mouse himself, running quickly along the pavement. He ran into a doorway as soon as he saw the car, because he was afraid of things that went along the road.

"There—see how scared he is!" said Noddy. "He would never dare to rob anyone. We won't stop to speak to him about the bell."

"Wait, little Noddy! Stop the car," said Tessie, suddenly. "He isn't wearing his bell. Let's ask him why."

So they called to the little mouse. "Why aren't you wearing the bell you bought at the bell-shop?"

The clockwork mouse squeaked at them, looking as scared as he always did. "I'm not wearing it because I didn't buy it for myself. I bought it for someone else," he said.

"WHO?" shouted Noddy and Tessie together and they frightened the mouse so much that he almost ran away.

"I bought it for the little toy soldier who lives at the wooden fort," said the mouse, trembling. "Don't shout at me like that. You'll make my whiskers fall off. Sammy the soldier asked me to buy him one and he gave  me sixpence. Why do you want to know?"

But Tessie and Noddy didn't answer! They drove to the fort at top speed. The wooden draw-bridge was up, and the sentry wouldn't let them past.

"We want to speak to Sammy the soldier!" said Noddy, but it wasn't a bit of good. The

sentry wouldn't let them into the fort. What a nuisance!

They drove back to Noddy's house and sat down to have some lemonade. "NOW what are we going to do?" said Noddy.

46

10

IN THE MIDDLE OF THE NIGHT

TESSIE Bear thought hard. Then she had a sip of lemonade. "Noddy, perhaps if it's Sammy the wooden soldier, he will break into somebody else's house tonight," she said. "We might catch him."

"But how should we know where to look?" asked Noddy.

"We could listen for his bell," said Tessie. "You'll have to wear your hat inside out so that your bell won't ring, else we shall keep thinking we hear Sammy's, and it will only be yours. Do let's creep out when it's dark, Noddy, and see if we can catch Sammy."

"You mustn't come," said Noddy. "You might get hurt."

"Oh, I'm not afraid," said Tessie. "And anyway, you can look after me, Noddy." And that made Noddy feel very brave indeed.

So they decided to wait until night-time and then see if the jingling of Sammy's bell would lead them to him. What an adventure!

"We'll have some supper first and then it will be dark and we'll go," said Noddy happily. It was so lovely to have dear little Tessie Bear there, his very own friend.

Tessie Bear was a very good cook. She fried some sausages beautifully, and she made a wonderful jam tart. Noddy said he had never tasted such a nice one in his life.

When it was dark, they set out together, Tessie's soft little paw inside Noddy's hand. They went up and down the streets, stopping to listen every now and again. And then they suddenly heard a bell jingling. Yes, they really did! Jingle-jingle-jingle it went, just like that.

"Where is it?" whispered Noddy.

"Over there in that garden," whispered Tessie, and they went in at the gate. "This is Miss Monkey's house and she's away!"

"Sh!" said Noddy, and stopped. Somebody was opening a window, his bell jingling softly. Now somebody was inside the house! Somebody was

48

NODDY AND TESSIE WENT IN AT THE GATE

opening the larder door and looking inside, feeling over the shelves!

"It must be Sammy Soldier!" whispered Noddy. "Stay here, Tessie. I'll catch him!"

So Noddy very boldly climbed in at the window too, but oh dear, Sammy heard him coming and

sprang at him. Down went little Noddy and banged his wooden head hard on the floor. Oooooh!

He caught hold of Sammy's leg and pulled him over. Sammy squealed and Noddy yelled. Good gracious, whatever was going on?

Tessie Bear was frightened. Was little Noddy being hurt? She ran into the road. "Help!" she cried. "Help, help! Won't somebody help?"

50

11
QUITE AN ADVENTURE

SOMEBODY was coming down the road on a bicycle, and standing on the bicycle step at the back was somebody else. Tessie heard the bicycle coming and saw its light. She shouted again.

"Oh, stop and help me, please! Do stop!"

The bicycle stopped, and the two people on it leapt off at once. "What's the matter?" asked a voice.

"Oh, little Noddy is in that house over there trying to catch a thief," said Tessie, beginning to cry. "And I think he's being hurt."

"Goodness me!" said the voice. Tessie couldn't see who it was in the dark, but she

liked the sound of the voice. "Come on, let's be quick!"

The two rushed to the window and climbed in, leaving Tessie standing outside, crying. What a noise she heard! Thump! Biff! Bang! Oooooooh! Ow! Biff-biff. Thumpity-thump!

Tessie got into the car. Oh dear—was little Noddy all right? She didn't have to wait long before the front door opened and out came four people. One was being dragged along, howling, jingling a bell all the time.

But it wasn't Noddy—it was Sammy the wooden soldier! Aha! He was properly caught, and it wasn't a bit of good his wearing a bell on his hat to pretend he was Noddy because they all knew that *he* was the thief, not little Noddy.

Noddy's bell was ringing now too, because he had turned his hat the right way out. He felt very proud of himself. "Where are you Tessie?" he called. "It's all right. We've got him. Thank you for getting help for me!"

OUT CAME FOUR PEOPLE

Noddy didn't know who had come to help him. It was pitch-dark inside the house, and all he knew was that two people had suddenly arrived and had pulled Sammy Soldier away from him and dragged him to the front door.

Noddy had followed after, feeling very shaken. Then Tessie called to him.

"Noddy! I'm here, in the car. The others have taken Sammy Soldier to the police-station, and we're to follow."

"Who were they?" asked Noddy, but Tessie didn't know. She hadn't been able to see them in the dark, and had just heard them call out that she was to tell Noddy to meet them at Mr Plod's.

"I hope I shall drive the car all right," said Noddy, getting in. "I feel a bit peculiar. Car, go carefully, please."

The car went very carefully indeed to the police-station. The door was open and light streamed out on to the pavement.

54

Voices came from inside as Tessie and Noddy got out of the car and went through the door.

And WHO do you think had come to help little Noddy in Miss Monkey's house? Guess!

Yes, you are right—it was dear old Big-Ears on his bicycle, with Little-Ears, his brother, riding behind on the step. Well, well, well, to think of that!

12

TOMORROW IS A LUCKY DAY!

WHEN Noddy saw Big-Ears and Little-Ears holding Sammy Soldier tightly between them, he gave a shout.

"Big-Ears! Oh, Big-Ears, I AM glad to see you. Why didn't you tell me you were going away? I've been in such trouble. DEAR Big-Ears, I am so very glad to see you!"

AND he gave Big-Ears such a hug that he almost squeezed the breath out of him.

"Ooooof!" said Big-Ears, panting. "You're worse than a bear, Noddy. What's been the trouble?"

So Noddy told him and when Big-Ears heard how Sammy Soldier had made such trouble for poor Noddy, he glared at him so fiercely that Sammy hid himself under the table in fright.

"And if it hadn't been for little Tessie Bear I would never have caught Sammy Soldier, and nobody would ever have spoken to me again, and Mr Plod would have taken me to prison," said Noddy, squeezing Tessie's paw.

"She deserves a kiss," said Big-Ears, beaming at Tessie. He gave her a great big kiss, and so did Little-Ears, who was really very like Big-Ears except that he had such tiny ears.

"I'm sorry I thought bad things about you, Noddy," said Mr Plod. "And I'm sure everyone else will be sorry too. It was the bell jingling that made us think it was you. Sammy Soldier will be punished for that."

"And so he should be," said Big-Ears in a voice that made poor Sammy Soldier dive under the table again.

"Come along," said Little-Ears. "I want my supper. Take Tessie Bear home, Noddy, and come along to the toadstool house with us."

57

NODDY GETS INTO TROUBLE

"And tomorrow we'll give Tessie a tea-party," said Big-Ears, "because she's so clever, and so kind. You're lucky to have a friend like Tessie, Noddy."

Noddy took Tessie home and gave her a good-night hug, and then went to the toadstool house. What a time he and Big-Ears and Little-Ears had! Little-Ears knew so many funny jokes and Noddy

laughed so much that he rolled off his chair seven times!

Tomorrow—ah, just you wait and see what happens tomorrow, little Noddy! There'll be a tea-party, of course—and everyone will come. What will they say to you?

"We're *so* sorry, Noddy, that we thought bad things of you! Please do forgive us!" That is what they will say. And they are going to bring Surprises for Noddy, to make up to him for all the horrid things they said.

Tessie will have Surprises too—a bow for her neck, a flower for her hat, and shoes with

58

WHAT A WONDERFUL PARTY!

bobbles on. What a wonderful party it will be. I shouldn't be surprised if a song comes into Noddy's head at the party, would you? How will it go? I think it might sound a bit like this:

"Oh this is going to be
A lucky day for me!
Surprises and a Party,
Hey-diddle-diddle-dee!
Big-Ears will be there,
And little Tessie Bear,
And Little-Ears as well,
Hey-diddle-diddle-dare!
And everyone will say,
'Is Noddy here today?
We've come to say we're sorry!'
Hey-diddle-diddle-day!
Oh this is going to be
A lucky day for me,
A happy day for Tessie,
Hey-diddle-diddle-dee!"